The Two Jacks first published in 1999 in Great Britain
Screw Loose first published in 1998 in Great Britain

Published in one volume as *Mixed Up Madness*
in 2007 in Great Britain by Barrington Stoke
18 Walker St, Edinburgh EH3 7LP

www.barringtonstoke.co.uk

ISBN: 978-1-84299-494-8

Printed in Great Britain by Bell & Bain Ltd

The Two Jacks

by

Tony Bradman

Illustrated by Ross Collins

For Jacks and Miss Wilsons
everywhere

Contents

Miss Wilson.

Jack Baker.

Jack Barker.

Chapter 1
Miss Wilson's First Day

This is the story of two boys called Jack, one supply teacher called Miss Wilson and a small mistake ... that changed each of their lives forever.

The two Jacks lived in the same street, went to the same school, were both in Mrs Heath's class and had surnames which were nearly the same. Only one letter was different. One was Jack BAKER and the other was Jack *Barker*.

Nobody had ever muddled them up, though. For a start, they looked very different. Jack BAKER was quite short for his age, had red hair and was softly spoken. Jack *Barker* was big and dark and had a loud voice.

They behaved differently, too. You know how every class has the same cast of characters in it? There's the Joker and the Shy One and the Worrier and the Tell-Tale and the Boaster and the Chatterer and the Weirdo and the Two Best Friends Who Argue All The Time. Well, Jack BAKER was the Perfect Pupil and Jack *Barker* was the Naughty Boy.

They had always been that way – or at least, that's what everybody thought. Jack BAKER was the boy with his hand up first. He was the boy with the right answer, the boy with top marks. Teachers could rely on him to take the register to the office. He was the polite boy who was asked to look after any important visitors.

Jack *Barker*, however, was the complete opposite of that. He was the boy who wouldn't put his hand up, the boy who refused to do his work, the rude and cheeky boy who always misbehaved. He was the boy who had to be kept out of the way when anybody important came to visit the school.

The two Jacks had never taken much notice of each other. Jack BAKER was too busy being The Perfect Pupil, and Jack *Barker* had his hands full being The Naughty Boy. They might have wondered if they could possibly have anything in common.

And that's how things would have stayed ... if it had not been for Miss Wilson.

Teachers come and teachers go, and halfway through this particular school year, one teacher went and another one came. Mrs Heath broke her leg playing football with the wild Year Six girls and she was taken to hospital.

So Mr Scott, the Head, had to find a supply teacher for Mrs Heath's class.

That supply teacher was Miss Wilson, who arrived at the school early the next morning. As usual, she felt quite nervous. In fact, she was starting to wonder whether she was really cut out to be a teacher. She couldn't seem to get a full-time job and the classes she taught were often difficult.

But then maybe that was her fault, she thought. The truth was … she didn't feel sure of herself in front of a class and perhaps the children could sense her nerves. It was something she'd been worrying about, anyway. The trouble was, the more she worried, the less confident she felt.

"Ah, welcome to our school, Miss Wilson," said Mr Scott and shook her hand. "I can't tell you how relieved I am to have you here. I didn't think we'd get anyone at such short notice.

Right, let me show you round before our charming little horrors turn up and battle commences. If you'd just like to follow me ..."

Mr Scott gave Miss Wilson a lightning tour of the school. There was a lot for her to take in. Mr Scott showed her the hall, and the classrooms, and the staffroom, and where the tea and coffee and chocolate biscuits were kept, and where the teachers' toilets were. Then the other teachers began to arrive.

Mr Scott introduced her to some of them, and some of them introduced themselves, and soon Miss Wilson's head was spinning with names and faces she couldn't keep together. Then suddenly it was time to make for the classrooms and she found herself scurrying behind Mr Scott towards hers.

"Er ... is there anything I should know about the class, Mr Scott?" she said, breathlessly. Mr Scott was marching down the corridor and it was hard to keep up. Miss Wilson could hear children laughing and shouting in the playground. "I mean, I would have liked to look at their records ..."

"Oh, they're a nice enough bunch," said Mr Scott, breezily. "All the usual characters, plus one bright, very helpful lad, Jack BAKER, and one real scallywag, Jack *Barker*. You ought to watch out for those two. Here's your prison cell ... see you at lunchtime, if you survive till then, ha ha!"

Mr Scott strode on towards his office and Miss Wilson went into her empty classroom. Just then she heard a loud whistle blast outside, and the children quietening down as they lined up to come in. She gulped. She would be meeting her class any minute. What was it Mr Scott had said?

Something about two boys she should watch out for, one called Jack BAKER and one called Jack *Barker*. One was very bright and one was very naughty. Her head was still spinning with the other teachers' names and for a second she couldn't remember which Jack was which.

Quick, quick, she thought, panicking slightly as she heard the children coming into the school. BAKER, *Barker*, bright, naughty, *Barker*, BAKER – yes, that was it, Jack *Barker* was the bright boy and Jack BAKER was the naughty one. Phew, she thought, it was a good job she'd got it sorted out.

But we know she hadn't. And *that*, of course, was the small mistake ...

Chapter 2
A Bit of a Mix-up

The children filed in and quietly took their usual seats. Jack BAKER was first into the room. His place was beside the door because he ran errands for Mrs Heath. Jack *Barker* rolled up last. His place was right next to Mrs Heath's desk because that was where she could keep an eye on him.

But as everybody knew, there was no Mrs Heath today. There was this new teacher instead, and that made the day more interesting before it had even really started. The children whispered to each other and stared wide-eyed at Miss Wilson. They waited to see what kind of a teacher she was going to be.

"Good morning, class," said Miss Wilson, nervously.

The class replied with a mumbled "Good morning, Miss."

"My name is Miss Wilson," she continued, "and I'll be, er ... looking after you while Mrs Heath is away. As far as Mr Scott is aware, she'll be off for at least a week, I'm afraid."

"She'll be all right, though, won't she?" said Kylie, the Worrier.

"Oh, I should think so," said Miss Wilson gently. She knew exactly what it was like to be someone who worried. "She just needs to get

some rest. I believe she's fine, apart from her leg, that is."

"It sounds bad if she's apart from her leg, Miss," said Jamie, the Joker.

He giggled at his own joke and looked round at the rest of the class. A few of the other children giggled too. Most of them, however, ignored him, and watched Miss Wilson closely to see how she would react.

"Very funny," she said … and smiled. So she wasn't going to be terribly strict, everybody thought. They relaxed a little. In fact, she seemed rather nervous. "But let's get on. We ought to begin by, er … taking the register."

And that's just what she did. She looked at each child in the class as they replied to their names, examining the two Jacks more carefully than the rest. Eventually she read out the last name, entered the last tick and closed the register. At once Jack BAKER jumped up from his seat.

"Shall I take it to the office, Miss?" he said eagerly. "I usually …"

"No thank you, Jack," said Miss Wilson quickly, the word 'naughty' instantly attaching itself to the name 'BAKER' in her brain. The last thing she needed on her first morning was for the register to go astray.

"I'd rather somebody else did that. Here you are, er ... Jack."

And so saying, she held the register out towards ... Jack *Barker*.

It was a strange moment for the class. Everybody's eyes were focused on the flat object in Miss Wilson's hand. An intense hush filled the room. The children waited expectantly. She was asking Jack *Barker* to take the register to the office and not Jack BAKER! The Naughty Boy, not the Perfect Pupil!

Well, it was as if the world had suddenly been turned upside down.

"Are you sure, Miss?" said Alice, The Tell-Tale. "Jack *Barker*'s ..."

"Sssh!" several children hissed at her. The rest of the class knew Alice was on the point of revealing that Jack was the Naughty Boy and they didn't want her to. They had all realised the day might become even more interesting ... Luckily, Miss Wilson didn't seem to have noticed.

"I'm positive," Miss Wilson said, deciding then and there to start as she intended to go on. That meant not allowing any of the children to argue with her. "Off you go, Jack *Barker*. I know I can trust you just by looking at your face. The rest of us will start on some worksheets ..."

Jack *Barker* could hardly believe what he had heard. He took the register from Miss Wilson as if he were in some kind of dream, stood up and walked towards the door. He paused and glanced back at Miss Wilson. She nodded to him, then carried on giving out the worksheets.

Jack BAKER was sitting in his seat nearby and for a second the two Jacks glanced at each other in surprise. Then Jack *Barker* opened the door and Jack BAKER wistfully watched him set off down the corridor.

"OK, has everybody got a worksheet?" Miss Wilson was saying. "Right, now pay attention ...

that includes you, Jack BAKER. Look at me, please."

Jack BAKER turned round, his face suddenly redder than his hair. Miss Wilson hadn't sounded particularly stern or cross. It had been more of a gentle reminder. All the same, it had come as a shock. Mrs Heath never had to make him pay attention and he suddenly felt distinctly unsettled.

Jack *Barker* was feeling the same. He was utterly amazed a teacher had asked *him* to do something responsible. He was even more amazed when he actually did it. He took the register to the office, he gave it to a very surprised secretary and – with only one detour – he came back to class.

It was definitely a different class from usual. The two Jacks might be unsettled, but everybody else was excited. Long before morning play, it was clear Miss Wilson had got the two Jacks muddled up. She thought Jack BAKER was the Naughty Boy, and Jack *Barker* was the Perfect Pupil.

The children glanced at each other and raised their eyebrows, whispered some more, and wondered how the two Jacks would react.

But before we find out, we need to know a bit more about them both ...

Chapter 3
Jack BAKER's Story

Jack BAKER hadn't always been the Perfect Pupil. When he'd started in the reception class with the other little ones, he'd been much the same as them. Sometimes he was good, and sometimes he was naughty, and he'd never thought about it. He just did what he did and that was it. But then his Dad had left home and hadn't come back.

Jack had been very small and hadn't really understood what was going on. All he knew was that one day his Dad was there ... and the next he wasn't and Jack was living alone with his Mum. It was as if half Jack's world had suddenly vanished and a gaping hole had appeared in its place.

Of course Jack had been very upset. He did what children often do when that kind of thing happens to them. He clung to his Mum, he began sucking his thumb again, he wet the bed, and he kept asking when his Dad would be back. The answer was always the same. Dad wasn't coming home.

But Jack did see him. For a while, his Dad took him to the park, or to McDonald's on Saturdays. Then his Dad missed a Saturday, and the next one, and the one after that. Then suddenly his Dad went to work in another part of the country, although he did phone Jack when he could.

And *then*, after six months ... the phone calls stopped as well.

In the end, Jack couldn't remember what his Dad looked like and he gave up talking about him. He stopped sucking his thumb and wetting the bed too. On the outside, he was happy enough. He loved his Mum, and his Mum loved him. She had a job, they had a nice flat, and they had fun.

But on the inside ... well, on the inside it was a different story.

Jack might not have mentioned his Dad, but he still thought about him. In fact, he thought about him a lot. Jack wondered what he was doing and why he never sent any birthday cards or Christmas cards or presents. But most of all, he wondered why his Dad had left home in the first place.

Jack knew his Mum was prettier than most of his schoolmates' Mums. She was a great cook, she got on with everybody, she was clever, and Jack reckoned she was probably very good at her job, too. Jack had decided long ago that his Dad couldn't possibly have gone because of his Mum.

So there was just one person whose fault it could have been.

Jack told himself that it must have been something about *him* that had made his Dad leave. For a time he had racked his brains trying to puzzle it out – was it something he had said, or done? Maybe he'd upset his Dad in some way. Maybe he hadn't been very good at his school work ...

But it was no use. Jack had no idea what the problem had been, and that worried him. What if his Dad came back and thought Jack was letting him down the same as ever? Why, he'd probably just leave again. And what if Jack did something his Mum didn't like? *What would happen then?*

He decided there was only one solution. He would simply have to be ... perfect. He would make sure he didn't do *anything* wrong, ever. So he helped his Mum at home and he never misbehaved with her. He worked as hard as he could at school, too, and never misbehaved there, either.

Of course, all the teachers said nice things about him and he liked that. And he liked the way they gave him important jobs to do. But he found out there was a dark side to being the Perfect Pupil. The other children were often horrible to him and called him 'boffin' and 'teacher's pet'.

Worse than that, Jack felt he could never relax. He constantly had to make sure he was doing his best and that the teachers were pleased with him. Once in a while Jack did think it might be good not to worry so much … but he would swiftly crush the thought and work even harder.

Then along came Miss Wilson and turned his world upside down.

Jack had been extra keen to impress her that morning. He felt it was important to get off to a good start with a new teacher and he'd been ready to be as helpful and hard-working as could be. But we know what happened … For Jack BAKER, the day got more and more difficult.

He had been *so* unsettled by losing his register job, and then by what Miss Wilson had said to him, that he had at once begun to worry. Long before morning play, the worry had become panic. It never occurred to him Miss Wilson might simply have muddled him up with Jack *Barker.*

Jack BAKER could not help thinking he must be doing something wrong. The panic made it hard for him to concentrate, so when he handed in his worksheet, he hadn't answered all the questions ... and he'd made quite a few mistakes. The rest of the class could hardly believe it. As Jack went back to his seat, he was so upset he didn't look where he was going ...

He bumped into the corner of Mrs Heath's desk, knocking over the vase of dried flowers that stood there. It fell to the floor and smashed. Jack looked down at the awful mess, then up at Miss Wilson's annoyed face.

"Oh, Jack," she said as the class held its breath, "you *are* naughty!"

Jack BAKER just didn't know what to say.

Chapter 4
Jack *Barker*'s Story

Jack *Barker* hadn't always been the Naughty Boy, either. When he'd started in the reception class with the other little ones, he'd been the same as them and Jack BAKER. In fact, he'd usually been good, and when he was naughty, he'd never been *that* naughty. He'd never had reason to be.

But then his Mum had suddenly become ill and died.

Jack had been very young at the time and he hadn't really understood what was going on. He remembered visits to the hospital, and his Mum not being able to speak to him, and his Dad coming home one day and telling him his Mum had gone. Jack didn't remember the funeral.

And of course, like Jack BAKER, Jack had been very upset, although he didn't do the same kind of things. Once the first few really bad weeks were over, he simply became very quiet and withdrawn. He worried for a while that *he* might become ill and die, just like his Mum.

He never talked to his Dad about it. He didn't know how to. Anyway, his Dad was very quiet and withdrawn himself. Then, after a couple of months, his Dad began to seem more cheerful. And then his Dad brought somebody home to meet Jack. It was Jill, a lady he worked with.

Then, a year later ... Jack's Dad and Jill were married.

Jack remembered the wedding. He remembered having to dress up in a fancy outfit, going to the registry office and running around inside a hall where there were lots of people. Most of them seemed to be happy and

laughing and, on the outside, Jack was happy and laughing too.

But on the inside ... well, on the inside, it was a different story.

Jack never mentioned his Mum but he still thought about her almost all the time. Quite often he wanted to talk about her to his Dad. But he didn't think his Dad would like the idea ... not now he had a new wife. Deep down, that made Jack feel angry with his Dad and his step-mum.

So he started being naughty with them, especially with his step-mum. She tried her best not to lose her temper, and they might have learned to get along OK ... but then she had a baby, a little girl. And then she had another little girl the next year, and another one the year after that.

All this made life pretty tough for Jack.

Babies are lovely and Jack was fond of his little sisters. But they kept his Dad and his step-mum very busy and very tired, and they didn't have much time for Jack. He'd grown bigger as well, and a bit clumsy, and once or twice he bumped into a highchair or hugged a sister slightly too hard.

He hadn't meant any harm, but it didn't seem to matter – he was still shouted at and told off. That made him feel even more angry with his Dad and his step-mum, so he started to misbehave a lot more. Then he started to misbehave at school as well. That led to even more tellings-off.

But the more tellings-off he got, the worse he behaved. Soon everybody, including Jack himself, had forgotten that he had ever been good. His Dad and his step-mum and his teachers expected him to be naughty. And that's exactly what he usually was, which only proved them right.

From time to time he heard some of the teachers saying hurtful things about him. Jack just shrugged and pretended not to care. He had found out that there was a not-so-bad-side to being the Naughty Boy. It was definitely a good way to make sure you got plenty of attention.

Jack also enjoyed having a reputation among the other kids. Once in a while he did wonder how it would feel to be liked by the teachers and not to be in trouble constantly ... but he would swiftly crush that thought and think of some new mischief to get up to.

Then along came Miss Wilson and turned his world upside down.

Jack hadn't been particularly interested in her that morning. If anything, he'd simply thought she would probably give him a hard time, exactly the same as his other teachers had done in the past: We know what happened ... and for Jack *Barker*, the day got more and more amazing.

He had been so unsettled by doing the register job and then by what Miss Wilson had said to him, that he began to think. She'd said she knew she could trust him *just by looking at his face* ... So on the way back from the office, he'd slipped into the boys' toilets to look in the mirror. Maybe Miss Wilson could see something others couldn't, he thought.

Back in class, he sat and studied his worksheet. Jack's usual way with worksheets was to draw rude pictures and scribble all over them and not answer any of the questions. Somehow he couldn't bring himself to behave like that with Miss Wilson ... He did his best to finish it.

When Jack BAKER knocked the vase over and was told off by Miss Wilson, Jack *Barker* raised his hand. Miss Wilson turned and smiled.

"Don't worry, Miss!" said Jack *Barker*. "I'll clear it up for you!"

"Oh, Jack," she said as the class breathed out, "you *are* good!"

Now *nobody* knew what to say.

Chapter 5
Miss Wilson Works it Out

There was silence for a moment, then Miss Wilson accepted Jack *Barker*'s offer. But she also told Jack BAKER to help him, and soon the two Jacks were gathering up the pieces of the smashed vase and the sorry-looking remains of Mrs Heath's dried flowers. They dumped the lot in her bin.

"OK, everybody," said Miss Wilson. She thanked Jack *Barker* and told Jack BAKER to be more careful in future. Both Jacks went back to their seats. "Now I've got a better idea of what you can do, I think we should try some maths. What textbook have you been using this term?"

And so the morning passed by, with Miss Wilson teaching and the class responding well, she thought. They weren't as difficult as other classes she'd taught and she relaxed a little. As Mr Scott had said, there were all the usual characters and Miss Wilson spotted most of them pretty quickly.

Kylie was the Worrier and Jamie was the Joker, of course. Alice was clearly the Tell-Tale, Darren was the Chatterer, Jasmine the Shy One, Sophie the Boaster, Elliott the Weirdo and Saffron and Mercedes were very definitely the Two Best Friends Who Argue All The Time.

It was going to be OK, Miss Wilson kept telling herself. But then, not long before lunchtime, doubt started to creep into her mind.

The class was rather ... quiet, she thought. Darren wasn't chattering, Jamie wasn't joking, Sophie wasn't boasting and Saffron and Mercedes weren't arguing.

There was a peculiar feeling in the classroom, a sense of the children waiting and being watchful ... They seemed slightly excited, too, almost as if they were hoping something interesting was going to happen at any moment. Miss Wilson certainly hadn't expected them to behave like that.

The two Jacks had surprised her even more.

Jack BAKER had knocked over the vase ... but now Miss Wilson came to think about it, she realised it might have been an accident. He hadn't done much else she could call naughty. He certainly hadn't shown himself to be – what was it Mr Scott had said? *A real scallywag.*

Then there was his worksheet. It had been surprisingly neat and tidy, and he'd got more of the questions right than anybody in the whole class. But oddly enough, he'd seemed quite upset that he'd made even a few mistakes. It was almost as if he'd wanted it to be perfect, she thought.

And Jack *Barker had* offered to clear up the mess after the vase had got knocked over ... but now Miss Wilson came to think about it, everybody else in the class had seemed amazed when he'd said it. Which seemed strange if he was usually – what was it Mr Scott had said? *Very helpful.*

Then there was *his* worksheet. It had been surprisingly messy and untidy and he'd got most of the questions wrong. But oddly enough, he'd seemed really pleased with himself when he'd handed it in. It was almost as if he couldn't believe that he'd managed to finish it at all.

Miss Wilson was still puzzling over the two Jacks when the bell went for lunchtime. She dismissed the class and most of the children dashed out. Jack BAKER hung back, looking at her with an anxious expression on his face and Jack *Barker* asked if he could do anything for her.

"Er ... no, I don't think so, Jack," she said. "You two boys run along."

It was chaos in the staffroom. Teachers were making tea and coffee. They were eating their sandwiches and chocolate biscuits, discussing the disasters that had happened during the morning and just generally gossiping. Miss Wilson found a seat in the corner and started on her own packed lunch.

"You survived then, Miss Wilson, ha ha!" said Mr Scott, sitting beside her. "And it seems you've made an excellent start. I don't know what you've done to Jack *Barker*. The secretary tells me he was as good as gold when he brought the register to the office. Keep up the good work!"

Mr Scott jumped to his feet and strode off before Miss Wilson had a chance to reply. Not that she wanted to. She sat there feeling distinctly unsettled, forgetting the half-eaten cheese sandwich in her hand. Mr Scott's words seemed to imply that Jack *Barker* wasn't always good ...

Miss Wilson began to wonder if she had made a small mistake.

By the end of the lunchtime break, she knew that was exactly what she had done. She chatted with the other teachers in the staffroom, and soon discovered they all had stories to tell about the naughty things Jack *Barker* had done – and they all had nice things to say about Jack BAKER, too.

Miss Wilson walked sadly back to her classroom, convinced now that she was the worst teacher in the world. She sat at her desk listening to the children laughing and shouting in the playground. She cursed herself for being so stupid. How could she have got the two Jacks muddled up?

She heard the whistle outside, and the children quietening down, and something else occurred to her. She had obviously upset Jack BAKER – but it seemed her mistake had made Jack *Barker* behave well for a change. So maybe – just maybe – it hadn't been such a bad thing after all ...

Chapter 6
A Fresh Start

For most of the class, that afternoon turned out to be a little disappointing. Miss Wilson soon made it clear she hadn't got the two Jacks muddled up anymore. She kept smiling at Jack BAKER and let him run several small errands, and she was rather wary of Jack *Barker* now.

So it seemed the world was turning the right way up again.

Jack BAKER was very relieved, although he still felt pretty anxious. That made him work even harder to impress Miss Wilson. And Jack *Barker* felt very confused. He began to wonder bitterly if Miss Wilson was just going to treat him the same as every other teacher did.

They were both in for a bit of a surprise. Miss Wilson didn't go straight home after school that day. She went to see the secretary and asked if she could have a look at the class records. She thought it might be a good idea to find out as much as she could about the two Jacks ...

She studied the records carefully. The next day, she asked her fellow teachers lots of questions. It wasn't long before she began to realise there was much more to Jack BAKER and Jack *Barker* than met the eye. Each had something in his past that might have made life difficult, to say the least.

It couldn't have been easy for Jack *Barker* to lose his Mum, she thought. It must have been even harder when that was swiftly followed by the arrival of a step-mum, then three baby sisters. And Jack BAKER was so worried the whole time about being perfect that he never seemed able to relax or have any fun.

Everybody always expected Jack *Barker* to be naughty and Jack BAKER to be perfect, she thought. So nobody ever gave them the chance to be any different. But they deserved that chance, Miss Wilson thought – and she was the person to make sure they got it. She started with Jack *Barker* ...

"Hang on a second, Jack," she said as the children were leaving the classroom at lunchtime. "Could I have a word?"

"Yes, Miss?" Jack mumbled. He paused by her desk, looking sullen. He couldn't remember doing anything naughty but he waited to be told off anyway.

"I need somebody to be, er ... paper monitor for the rest of the week," said Miss Wilson. "And I was wondering ... if you'd like to do the job?"

"Er ... *me*, Miss?" said a stunned Jack.

"Yes, *you*, Jack," she said and laughed. "Try not to look so shocked. It'll do you good to have some responsibility. Well, what do you say?"

"Thanks, Miss!" said Jack with a huge grin. "I won't let you down!"

He didn't, either. That afternoon and for the next few days, Jack *Barker* was the best paper monitor the class had seen. He was so grateful to Miss Wilson for giving him the opportunity, he felt even less willing to let her down in his work. So, amazingly, he kept doing his best with that, too.

Not that he changed completely. Old habits die hard, and Jack had been too naughty for too long to become well behaved *that* quickly. But the entire school noticed he was a lot less naughty than usual. And when he *did* misbehave, it was more cheeky and funny than really bad.

Sorting Jack BAKER out was rather more difficult, though.

Miss Wilson tried getting him to relax and not worry so much about being perfect. But she could see she wasn't having much effect on him. Then, on her third day with the class, she heard Jack *Barker* being a bit cheeky to another teacher after assembly and had an idea ...

"Hang on a second, Jack," she said to Jack BAKER as the children were leaving the classroom at the end of school. "Could I have a word?"

"Yes, Miss?" Jack squeaked anxiously, pausing by the door. He didn't think he'd done anything wrong but he still felt very worried anyway.

"I'd like you to sit next to Jack *Barker* from tomorrow, Jack," she said. "You'll be able to, er ... help me more if you're sitting closer to my desk."

"Will I, Miss?" said a slightly happier Jack.

"Yes, Jack," said Miss Wilson and laughed. "I think it'll do you good to be near someone who knows how to have fun. And, one more thing, don't worry, OK?"

"No, Miss," said Jack with an uncertain smile. "I'll try not to."

The next morning, Miss Wilson could tell that putting the two Jacks together was going to help them both. Jack BAKER could help Jack *Barker* with his school work, and Jack *Barker* could help Jack BAKER to relax and enjoy life a little more. It still wouldn't be easy for either of them ...

Miss Wilson wished she could stay longer. But this was her last day, so she was leaving just when she was beginning to realise she might make a real difference – and that she might be a better teacher than she'd thought.

Suddenly the classroom door opened and in came Mr Scott.

"Ah, Miss Wilson," he whispered. "It seems Mrs Heath will be off for a while yet so I was wondering if you'd stay with us till the end of term, at least. And did I, er ... mention she was going to leave at the end of the year, too?"

Miss Wilson glanced at the two Jacks and smiled, and they smiled back.

Sometimes in life, just as in stories, things really do work out OK ...

MEET THE AUTHOR – TONY BRADMAN

What is your favourite animal?
Whales
What is your favourite boy's name?
Thomas (my son's name)
What is your favourite girl's name?
**Sally, Emma and Helen
(my wife and daughters)**

What is your favourite food?
Grilled fish
What is your favourite music?
The Beatles
What is your favourite hobby?
Going to the cinema

MEET THE ILLUSTRATOR – ROSS COLLINS

What is your favourite animal?
Manatees
What is your favourite boy's name?
Connor
What is your favourite girl's name?
Wednesday
What is your favourite food?
Steak – medium rare
What is your favourite music?
Southern Swing
What is your favourite hobby?
Deep Sea pearl fishing

Turn the page
for more ...

MIXED
UP
MADNESS!

Screw Loose

Written and illustrated

by

Alison Prince

To all those who have ever wished
things were different

Contents

Chapter 1
The Screwdriver

Roddy Watt found the screwdriver by the school gate. It was lying on the tarmac. It was a short, strong screwdriver with a stubby handle, just the right size to fit into his pocket.

He unscrewed a coat-hook in the cloakroom with no bother at all, and smiled. Then he put the screwdriver back in his pocket and went upstairs for registration.

Nobody had seen him, because he was late, as usual.

"Roderick Watt, you are late, as usual," said his class teacher, Mrs Bigg.

"That's right, Miss," agreed Roddy. "Sorry."

Mrs Bigg sighed and asked, "Why are you always late?"

"Dunno," said Roddy.

Wasn't it obvious? Nobody in their right mind would want to come into this place with its stupid baby-blue paint and its posters about drug-taking. Who would want to spend a day being bored?

It was better to hang about a bit on the way and go into the shop with the *Daily Record* posters outside before he got on the bus. He often took some time choosing

which crisps to buy and what kind of chewing gum. Still, he had the screwdriver now. That would make things more interesting.

"I might be early tomorrow," he said.

"Oh good," said Mrs Bigg.

Roddy was in school the next day before anyone else. He unscrewed a notice on the Head's door, a window-catch or two and the hinges to the door of the boys' toilet. He slackened off the brackets that held up the shelves in his classroom.

The door opened as he was dealing with a couple of tables. Biff came in with her usual armful of magazines. "Hi," she said. "Why are you so early?"

"Just thought I'd have a change," said Roddy. "Why are *you* early?"

"My Mum does an early-morning job at the hospital," Biff said. "Cleaning. So I go with her before school. That's where I get the magazines. People give loads of them to the hospital, and the nurse chucks out the old ones. New ones, too, if they're sexy or about motorbikes and things."

She dumped her armful on the nearest table, which lurched and fell sideways. "This place makes you sick," she said. "Why don't they spend some money on it?"

Roddy tried not to look guilty.

"The leg's come unscrewed," he said as he picked the table up. He fished the screwdriver out of his pocket and hoped Biff would not notice that the screws were in there as well. But she did, of course.

"So that's why you were so early," she said. "Hey, was it you who undid the KNOCK

AND WAIT notice off Mr Pimm's door? I saw it lying on the floor."

"Could have been," said Roddy and shrugged.

Biff laughed. "Great!" she said. "Wait till I tell Debbie and Sheena!"

"Give me a break," said Roddy. "Don't go telling everyone. If the jannie gets to know, I'm dead."

"What's a jannie?" asked a voice from the door.

Roddy and Biff turned to see Tim Tomkins standing there, with his floppy, fair hair falling over one eye. Tim had just come to Glasgow from London, and didn't know anything about anything.

"It's the janitor," Biff told him. "He looks after the building, does the boilers and that. Or sometimes the janitor's a she."

"Is that the guy called Mr Rundle?" asked Tim. "Wears a navy uniform, got that little office near the bogs?"

"That's right," said Roddy.

"So what mustn't he get to know?" Tim asked.

"Nothing," said Biff and Roddy together.

Tim nodded a couple of times. Then he wandered over to his place and sat down. He looked so miserable that after a few minutes they told him about the screwdriver. But Roddy threatened fatal damage to his Game Boy if he let on.

Chapter 2
Mr Rundle

The usual crowd was milling round the chip van at lunchbreak. Roddy went into the boys' toilet to do some more unscrewing. He found Mr Rundle busy replacing the door hinges.

"You're supposed to be outside," said Mr Rundle.

"I just needed a pee," said Roddy.

"On you go, then."

Roddy didn't need a pee at all, and found it difficult to produce much with Mr Rundle watching him.

"What's the matter with the door?" Roddy asked, in an innocent voice.

"We're having an attack of deconstruction," said Mr Rundle.

"What's that?"

Mr Rundle sighed. "Don't they teach you anything these days? Construction is putting things together, right? Deconstruction is taking them apart. Somebody around here has been taking things apart."

"Go on?" said Roddy.

Mr Rundle fixed him with an accusing eye. "And what's more, one of my screwdrivers is missing. Short one, with a stubby handle. You've not seen it, have you?"

"No!" Roddy's voice sounded a bit squeaky, even to himself.

"I'll be wanting it returned," said Mr Rundle.

And as Roddy went out, trying to look casual, he felt Mr Rundle's gaze drilling into his back.

After that, unscrewing things became a risky game, although it was fun. Roddy knew he was giving Mr Rundle a lot of work, but it was so great to have a real interest in school that he couldn't stop.

He watched carefully to make sure nobody was about before loosening desk legs and notice boards and the framed portrait of some old bird who had been the first Headteacher of the school.

Roddy was extra proud of this, because the portrait hung just outside the office of the present Head, Mr Pimm. He was a thin, stiff man who did not understand jokes. He wore a dark, blue suit with pin stripes, and Roddy thought he looked just like a Bic biro.

Mr Pimm seemed to get even thinner as the unscrewing epidemic went on. He kept bleating in Assembly about the tide of vandalism engulfing the school. He would nervously snatch his glasses off and on and run his fingers through what was left of his hair.

Roddy was glad the Head did not have the sense to offer a reward for information, because the secret was well and truly out now. Somebody would have cracked then and there if the money had been right. Dave Boyle's gang, who did most of the graffiti and general destruction, were

15

really annoyed that they had not thought of it first.

Stupid Joe Picken had a go at it, but he used a huge, great screwdriver that fell out of his sports bag in Media Studies. He got suspended, of course, but he didn't mind, because it gave him more time for his shoplifting. And Mr Pimm was even more upset when the unscrewing still did not stop.

Mr Pimm called in the Crime Prevention Officer (CPO for short) to talk to the school at Assembly. The CPO looked a bit like a social worker, Roddy thought, with a sports jacket over his police trousers. He went on about how awful it was to enter a life of crime.

Dave Boyle's gang were so interested that they hardly made any noise. But when Mr Pimm stepped to the lectern to thank the CPO, the top of it fell off. It hit him on the big toe. He stood there on one foot, trying not to hop, while everyone fell off their chairs laughing. It was one of Roddy's absolute triumphs, and even the Crime Prevention Officer was grinning, though he blew his nose to try and hide it.

Chapter 3
Wanted

The next morning, Mr Rundle was waiting in a van outside the entry to Roddy's flat.

"You're wanted," he said through the van's open window. "Get in."

"Wanted?" Roddy's heart thumped.

So the game was up. If you were wanted, it had to mean the police.

"Where are we going?" he asked, trying to sound calm.

"School, of course. But they asked me to have a word with you first."

Mr Rundle glanced over his shoulder, put the van in gear and set off down the road.

"You see, Mr Pimm's been taken ill."

"What sort of ill?"

"Mental. His wife phoned this morning to say he was under the table, barking. You've to take over."

Roddy frowned.

"What d'you mean, take over?"

"What I say. You're to be the new Head. They had the good sense to come to me, I'm glad to say. 'Mr Rundle', they said, 'if there's one person in a school who knows the score, it's the jannie'. Right enough, of course. So I suggested you."

This could not be real, Roddy thought. *Why me, why*? But at the back of his mind, he knew why.

Mr Rundle stopped at traffic lights and turned to look at him. "I know you, son," he said. "Like they say, you don't have to be mad to be a Head, but it helps. And you've a bit of a screw loose, as you might say. Right?"

Roddy felt his face redden. Mr Rundle held out his hand and said, "You'd best give me that screwdriver before we get any further. Could be tricky if you got caught with it. You being the Head and all."

Roddy fished in his pocket for the short, stubby screwdriver. He would miss it.

"Thanks," said Mr Rundle, dropping it into his own pocket. "I've missed that."

Roddy nodded. He understood how he felt. "Sorry," he said.

"That's all right." The jannie drove on.

As they neared the school, Roddy said, "I'm not dreaming, am I?"

"You could be," said Mr Rundle. "All I know is, I'm not."

Panic hit Roddy as if he had stepped out of an aeroplane at two thousand feet.

"I can't do this," he said desperately. "Run the school? You must be joking, aren't you? Tell me you are."

"No," said Mr Rundle. "I'm not joking. It's a stupid idea, I'll give you that, and I told them so, but that's what they want. Try it out, they said. When all the usual things fail, experiment with something new."

"But what'll I *do*?" shrieked Roddy.

"Anything you like. You're not allowed to sack the teachers, though. Not yet. You can do that later if you like, but it takes time to cook up the excuses."

Roddy nodded, thinking fast. "Does everyone know it's me in charge?"

"Your name's on the office door," said Mr Rundle. "And the staff have been told. You might find Mr Harris helpful."

He swung into the car-park behind the boiler room and switched the engine off.

Chapter 4
The Head

Roddy saw the neat, new name-plate on the door of the Head's office –
MR RODERICK WATT, HEADMASTER.

"I'll be calling you Mr Watt in future," Mr Rundle said, as he ushered him in. "At least, in front of the kids."

Roddy crossed to the desk with a leather top and sat down behind it. He felt very small.

"What'll I do?" he asked again and knew the question sounded pathetic.

"Have a meeting," advised Mr Rundle. "That's what they all do when in doubt. If you want to talk to the school, the button beside the mike on your desk is the PA. Public Address System," he added, as Roddy looked blank. "Best of luck."

And he went out, shutting the door behind him.

Roddy spun about in the big office chair. He found that it would spin right round if he gave himself a good push off, and he did that a couple of times. Then he became aware of the noise which drifted up through the window.

The school was outside, waiting for the bell that would ring in a couple of minutes.

Biff would be in the classroom already, getting her magazines organised for a day's reading. Tim too, probably, because he thought Biff was wonderful. And Dave Boyle's lot might be absolutely anywhere.

Roddy's tummy lurched uneasily as he thought about Dave Boyle. The bell rang, and he heard the hubbub grow louder as people poured into the building. He wished he was one of them, instead of being stuck here on his own.

A meeting, yes, that was the thing. He needed Biff in here. She was sensible, even if she did read magazines all the time. He needed one or two of the others as well. He pressed the button beside the microphone and said, "Hello?"

His voice echoed back from the corridor outside.

For a moment, he panicked. What was Biff's real name? He must do this properly. He tried again.

"Will Barbara Irene Ferris please come to the Headmaster's office at once," he said. "And Tim Tomkins."

Then he added, "Biff can bring some friends if she likes. And Dave Boyle and his lot had better come too."

But then there would be too many trouble-makers, so he said, "In fact, anyone from Mrs Bigg's class can come if they're interested."

The noise seemed to get more instead of less, and Roddy realised that none of the other classes knew what they were supposed to do.

He pressed the button once more. "Quiet!" he commanded. "And listen."

After a moment, he went on.

"Stay in your own classrooms for the first two periods. Discuss how you would like the school to be run, and write down some sensible notes. Use someone with decent handwriting. I don't want any scribbles from teachers. Bring the notes to my office at interval time, and I'll tell you then what to do next. Thank you."

Biff was the first to come tumbling in through the office door.

She was followed by Dave Boyle who was doubled up. He was cursing loudly that she had kicked him somewhere painful.

"Shut up and sit down," Roddy said bravely.

Dave stared at him.

"Who're you telling to – "

"SIT DOWN!" Roddy bellowed. "We can't muck about, there are things to do."

Dave grabbed one of the few chairs. He turned it the wrong way round and sat astride it, leaning his arms on the back.

"Go on then, big man," he sneered. "While we let you."

His gang grinned and nodded.

The whole of Mrs Bigg's class was piling into the room. At first it was bedlam, everyone talking at once and offering ideas.

Roddy found a notepad and scribbled hard, trying to get it all down. Debbie wanted to know why they should not eat in class, and Stewart said school should start at eleven and end at two, with an hour for lunch. Mike wanted to learn Greek.

A lot of people said teachers must not be sarcastic. Jenny said she would never get to university because you couldn't learn anything when people mucked about all the time. A lot of people agreed, but Dave Boyle's lot shouted them down. Danny didn't see why he had been banned from computing just because he had hacked into the school system.

Also, he had used the sports allowance to bet on his Dad's greyhound. He had replaced the money when it won, hadn't he? Plus a share of the profit – they ought to be grateful.

Everyone was fed up about not being able to sack the teachers but Sheena said, "Mrs Bigg's all right. She's strict, but you can see she likes us, really."

"Mr Crawley should go," said Stewart. "My mum says he doesn't correct half my spelling mistakes. How are you to know when it's wrong? No point in bothering."

Dave's lot shouted and laughed so much that Roddy couldn't hear half of what people said, and at last Biff yelled, "Look, SHUT UP!"

Then she said to Roddy, "The worst of the problem is THEM, the trouble-makers. They ruin everything. Lessons are dead boring because the teachers spend their whole time trying to cope with them. We ought to chuck them out."

"You can't, you stupid cow," said Dave. "It's the law. Think I'd be here two minutes if I didn't have to be?"

Uproar broke out again.

"LISTEN!" roared Roddy. When they were quieter he went on. "What if we take Mr Harris off all other classes and put him in permanent charge of the trouble-makers?"

"Brilliant," said Biff, amid shouts of protest.

"Harris is a monster," yelled Kevin, but a boy called Peter shook his head.

"He's tough, but he's fair," he said. "When it was snowing last year and I got my jacket stolen, he lent me one he had in the back of his car."

At that moment, Mr Rundle put his head round the door. He looked at Roddy Watt and said, "All right, Mr Watt? Anything I can do?"

"Can I hold your hand, Mr Watt?" mocked Dave. "Can I wipe your bum, Mr Watt?"

"There is something you can do," Roddy said to Mr Rundle. "We've decided to hand some of these people over to Mr Harris, full-time. So could you take them down to Mr Harris's room and give him this note?"

He scribbled busily. "Tell him the class he's got now can come up here – I'll look after them until we can get things sorted out."

"Right," said Mr Rundle. "I take it that'll be Dave Boyle and his lot?"

He glanced across the room and added, "I'll also take that boy who's scribbling on the telephone directory, and those two girls shouting out of the window. Over here by the door, please."

Somehow there was no arguing with Mr Rundle.

"Wow!" said Biff when the door closed. "Isn't it quiet!"

"It's going to stay that way," said Roddy.

He worked harder for the rest of the day than he had ever done in his life. Biff and the others wanted big changes. They wanted a 'self-service' timetable which let everyone choose from the lessons on offer. They also wanted help for Mr Harris in running his Sin Bin.

They asked for an agreement that anyone seriously mucking about in any other class would be sent to Mr Harris at once. And there would be a new deal with the staff, promising no chewing gum in class and no cheek, in exchange for prompt marking of work and a let-up on the sarcastic remarks.

Roddy struggled to write all this down in some sort of form that made sense. He didn't know if it would work or not. But at least it was worth a try.

At lunchbreak, he was too busy reorganising Mr Harris's class to go down to the canteen or out to the chip van. A pile of notes arrived from all the classes. His secretary came in and said she would type them out for him. She said he needed a break for a coffee and a sandwich.

"You'll have to learn to take it easy," she told him, "or you'll end up like poor Mr Pimm."

Roddy was late home because he had called a meeting with the staff to explain the new arrangements. Some of them had been really awkward and argued a lot. He staggered in through the door and collapsed in a chair.

"What have you been up to?" his mother asked.

Roddy explained. His mother smiled and said it must be some sort of project. She and Roddy's father were both teachers themselves, so they tended to talk a lot about things like projects. Roddy was too tired to argue.

He just about managed to eat his tea before going upstairs to bed. In the bathroom, he was amazed to see the face gazing back at him from the mirror looking so old and tired.

Chapter 5
Mystery

Next morning, Mr Rundle was not waiting outside in the van. Roddy got the early bus to school and made his way wearily to the office.

"And where are you going?" asked Mr Rundle, appearing behind him.

"Into the office. I mean – "

"No, you're not, son. Not unless you've been sent for."

"But – " Roddy looked at the name-plate on the door, MR RODERICK WATT, HEADMASTER. "Yesterday, I – "

"Yesterday, we had a new Head. Same name as you." Mr Rundle agreed. "He's still here today. You wouldn't know, of course, since you took the day off. Bunking off school, were you?"

"No!" said Roddy indignantly. "You know I wasn't. I was here. I was working really hard."

Mr Rundle glanced up and down the empty corridor. Then he said quietly, "We understand each other, son, don't we? Things will be different from now, you'll see. Now, away you go – and don't worry."

Then he knocked, opened the office door and went in, closing it behind him.

Roddy caught a brief glimpse of the new Head who was sitting in the swivel chair behind the desk. His face looked old and tired, just as Roddy's face had done when he saw it in the mirror last night.

Roddy turned away, his mind reeling. Biff was coming through the door.

"Hi!" she said. "Where were you yesterday? We've got this new Head. He's terrific. He's changing everything. And he's got the same name as you!"

"I know," said Roddy.

"Do you?" She seemed surprised. "Oh, OK then, I won't bother telling you."

Then she thought of something.

"You'd better stop the unscrewing, or you'll end up with Dave Boyle and that lot in Mr Harris's room. This Mr Watt's a lot tougher than old Pimm was. He's nice, though. We all like him."

"I'm glad," said Roddy.

He went down the corridor to the cloakroom. He was not sure if he was disappointed or relieved. What on earth had happened yesterday? Had he been dreaming? Who was the man in the office who shared his name?

It was crazy to think that there were two Roderick Watts. Could they have been the same person, just for one day?

The door of Mr Rundle's office stood open, as if on purpose. Roddy stopped and looked in. The short, stubby screwdriver

was lying on the table in a clear space of its own.

A creepy feeling came over Roddy. He remembered when Mr Rundle had reached out for it in the van.

Mr Rundle had said, "Could be tricky if you got caught with it, being the Head and all."

So he was not dreaming, yesterday *had* happened.

Roddy went on into the cloakroom and hung up his jacket. He felt strangely light and new. He found himself smiling. If he could run a school, he could do anything.

He heard the hubbub of people waiting for the bell. The new Head in his office would be hearing it, too. *The best of luck*, Roddy thought. *I gave you a good start, anyway.* Then he set out along the corridor to take his place in Mrs Bigg's classroom.

If you loved this,
why don't you try ...

The Dirty Dozen
by Tony Bradman

Ninety minutes. Two teams. One chance to win ...

Robbie wants to play for the coolest team in town, Top Grove FC. But first Top Grove want to see him play – in his own team. The problem is, he hasn't got one! Can Robbie get a squad into shape and onto the pitch?

You can order *The Dirty Dozen* directly from our website at www.barringtonstoke.co.uk

If you loved this, why don't you try ...

Get That Ghost To Go! by Catherine MacPhail

What would it be like to be haunted by a real ghost? Duncan doesn't know what's hit him when Dean's ghost begins to follow him everywhere. Dean chases dogs and upsets the teachers but no one else can see him. So Duncan gets the blame! How on earth can Duncan and his friends get that ghost to go?

You can order *Get That Ghost To Go* directly from our website at www.barringtonstoke.co.uk

If you loved this,
why don't you try ...

Game Boy
by Alan Durant

JP loves his Game Boy and he can't wait to try out his new game. But, as it starts, a strange message appears. JP finds himself in a thrilling life and death adventure and there's no going back. Can he get past the dangers – or will it be GAME OVER?

You can order *Game Boy* directly from our website at www.barringtonstoke.co.uk